SONS FOR KING YAH

SONS FOR KING YAH

BY LINDA HOWARD

illustrated by Ati Forberg

Logos International — Plainfield, New Jersey

Copyright© 1975 by Logos International
185 North Avenue, Plainfield, NJ 07060
All rights reserved
Library of Congress Catalog Card Number: 75-7480
International Standard Book Number: 0-88270-120-7
Printed in the United States of America

TO FRANK

Contents

The Two Kingdoms and the Prince	3
Dark Friday	8
The King's Surprise	14
The Secret Plan	19
Charis	27
Victor	36
The Mysterious Hill	42
What Victor Saw on the Hill	45
Final Instructions	49
The River of Death	53
Arrival at Joy Street	63
"Imp" Patient	68
Victor Finds a Pet	76
A Close Call	82
Wedding Bells	87

PART I

THE KINGDOM OF LIGHT

The Two Kingdoms and the Prince

Finding sons for King Yah was very hard. It often puzzled the Palace servants of the King. How could lowly peasants possibly turn down such a high, high honor? Yet, day after day, when the Ambassador approached the peasants, they would only laugh or curse scornfully, then turn and walk away.

It was hard for the Ambassador. He was the most gentle of all the Kingdom. He had a love for these peasants that was unbelievable. He was kind and meek. Even though he was laughed at, he would go back again and again to inquire if perhaps today the peasants would come with him into the Kingdom of Light to become sons of the glorious King Yah.

The Ambassador, too, was a source of wonder for the servants in the palace. How could someone of equal rank and honor to King Yah submit himself to such treatment — and from lowly peasants, too?

The Palace servants often talked about the three mighty and powerful rulers of the land. They were the King, the Prince and the Ambassador. Their story was interesting, but the servants could not understand it.

The Kingdom of Light had been a wonderful place for many years. The King was so good and kind to his subjects. His son, Prince Christos, had ruled with the King. The people were not peasants then. They were prosperous businessmen. Things went well for everyone in the Kingdom. Then, one day, the King's own prime minister had started a rebellion. He had first convinced some of the King's Palace servants to go with him. Then, cunningly, he had convinced the King's subjects to go across the River of Death. There he had set up the Kingdom of Darkness. The prime minister had become known as King Beel. He had started his kingdom on lies. Surely, he knew he could never be as mighty and powerful as King Yah. But he had a great power of persuasion. If anyone would take the time to listen to him, they would become spellbound. Soon they would believe his lies. His greatest lie was that he would make all the subjects kings. He would cunningly whisper to each man, "You will be great, greater than King Yah. Why, you are just as good as he is. What has he done that is so great? Come with me. Come into my kingdom. I will make you a king. We will be a kingdom of kings. We will be all powerful. Come with me."

Again and again, King Beel would tell his lies. Again and again, the subjects would follow him. The servants of the King could not understand. How could anyone believe that crafty and dishonest King Beel. Everyone knew that he was a liar.

An even greater mystery was the reaction of King Yah. The Palace servants had expected him immediately to attack the Kingdom of Darkness. Why, he had the mightiest army in all the world. He could easily destroy King Beel's army and his entire kingdom in one day. But he did not. Though very sad about the rebellion, he remained calm and unshaken by the events. The beginning of the rebellion had been the greatest blow of all. A dear friend of King Yah, a man named Adam Bloodman, was the first to cross the River of Death to join forces with King Beel.

Adam Bloodman had been the King's head gardener. This was a coveted position of high honor. Daily the gardener and his beautiful wife, Eve, would walk with the King through the gardens. They discussed many things, not only about the garden but also about the entire Kingdom and the people. King Beel was known to brag about the way he had reached Adam Bloodman. He first convinced Eve,

Adam's wife, that King Yah had not been completely honest with them.

As Eve began to listen to his cunning lies, she became restless and decided to try to find a way to "better herself" (as King Beel had put it). Soon she wanted desperately to join forces with King Beel. After that, Adam was easily convinced. And, so, the fateful day came when Adam Bloodman followed his wife across the river into the Kingdom of Darkness.

That very day a secret conference was held between the King, the Prince and the Ambassador. Something would be done. A plan was devised. It was a unique, complex, and daring plan. No one would know the details. But it soon became known the Prince had decided to pay a visit to the Kingdom of Darkness. "How could this help?" asked the Palace servants. "Why, wicked King Beel would only have him beaten, or something worse." Every servant in the Palace knew the life of their precious Prince was in grave danger though not one dared to speak openly about it.

The visit was planned for a time in the future. Only the three rulers knew for certain when it would be. In the meantime, messengers were sent from the Kingdom of Light over to the Kingdom of Darkness. They went to try to convince the subjects, now poor peasants, that they should cross the river once again and come back into the safety and prosperity of the

Kingdom of Light. Some peasants did come back. But each time the fate of the messengers was the same. They were beaten, some even killed, before they could return to King Yah.

The time for the Prince's trip began to draw near. Many of the Palace servants wanted to go with Prince Christos. He was the ruling Prince. Surely he would need them. They would take care of his every need. They would be sure he was not harmed, too. The servants were only waiting for the call from the King to volunteer. But the call never came. The Prince was to make the trip alone.

Then they learned that the day had arrived. The Prince would go on his journey. The King, Prince and Ambassador seemed almost pleased about the trip. It was like they knew a secret that no one else knew.

The plans for the journey were detailed. The three rulers had devised a clever disguise for the Prince. He would go to live in a lowly home. All this seemed foolish to the Palace servants, but they had long ago learned to trust the wisdom of their King.

Dark Friday

How lonesome the Kingdom of Light was without the Prince. His presence had put a special glow on everything and everyone. He seemed to know everyone in the Kingdom. Young children came to him at an early age. He would play with them for awhile. Then it seemed they would always end up in the Throne Room of his Father. There the children would sit with the three rulers. It was amazing they never seemed to get too busy with the details of State so that they could spend some time with everyone who came to see them. Some people would stay only minutes, some longer. Everyone who came first had to see the Prince. Then the Prince would take them to his Father.

Although the King, Prince and Ambassador were joint rulers they had separate functions. The King dealt with the matters of State primarily. He

held court. He saw that justice was performed. The Prince had been responsible for the people. His love for them was boundless. He was always there to meet the smallest needs. All you had to do was to take that need to him. He always had an answer.

But now, he had gone to the Kingdom of Darkness. The Palace servants contented themselves with the fact that those poor peasants were much more in need than they were. How those foolish peasants could be so blind, the servants did not know; but the truth was that they were. Therefore, the Prince was the very one, indeed the only one, to help them see the truth about King Beel.

Days and weeks slipped by. How long had it been since the Prince had left? One day without him in the Kingdom of Light seemed like an eternity. How long had it been? Several years had surely passed or had it been longer? During his absence the Prince had lived in obscurity in the humble little home. The Prince and King had worked out a system by which the Ambassador could keep in constant touch with both of them. Therefore, the King could reach the Prince at any time and the Prince was always in touch with the King. How this was no one seemed to know. All that was known for sure was it worked. There was no doubt the Ambassador was kept very busy, for the Prince and King were always in contact with one another.

Dark Friday

One day when the Kingdom of Light seemed especially glum without the Prince, a rumor began to spread. The time had come for the Prince to begin his mission there in the Kingdom of Darkness. What a joyous day that became, for soon the Prince would be back home where he belonged.

The Prince began to teach and tell everyone about the Kingdom of Light. He went everywhere telling the peasants about his Father. Some of the peasants were eager to hear about that wonderful Kingdom. But many did not like to hear about such things. They were sure the Prince had come to change everything and, indeed, he had. But they were the people who looked upon every change as something evil.

The Prince began to speak more boldly. Now, more and more people were beginning to follow him. This made the city leaders very angry. King Beel had many very devoted followers. They were not devoted because they loved him. They hated him and he, in turn, hated them. Yet they obeyed him without question. For he had promised them a kingdom and they had believed his lie.

Day after day, the reports in King Yah's Palace grew darker. King Beel had plotted to kill the Prince again and again. Each plot had failed. Because of their deep love and concern for Prince Christos, the Palace servants asked the King about the fearful reports. He always confirmed the reports. He told them he was keeping up with all of the details. Everything was going according to their plans and soon everything would be over. The Prince would be home again.

One Friday at exactly three o'clock a most terrible thing happened. The Kingdom of Light suddenly became dark, very dark. What had happened? What could it be? Then a most dreadful report began to spread. The Prince was dead. Could it be? No! No! Not our beloved Prince, not our lovely ruler!

How, oh how? It was the work of King Beel, of course. At last he had succeeded. Though no one in the Kingdom of Light wanted to believe it, they knew their lovely Prince had most certainly been killed. Even the sky knew, for all the light was gone. And with the light, all hope had gone, too.

What about the King and the Ambassador? Did they know? They so loved the Prince. "The news will kill them!" someone spoke out. The crowd grew silent. Yes. This news, the Prince's death, would most certainly kill them. The King loved his son so very much. He would certainly die from a broken heart. Everyone knew the King had wanted many, many sons. There had been talk some years ago that the King had plans to adopt children sometime in the future. But a little-known law had made such adoptions impossible. Now even Prince Christos was dead.

The Ambassador, too, how he loved the Prince and the King. That quiet, gentle Ambassador! He could not bear such a terrible blow. His heart, too, would break.

Would King Beel win after all? Would they, too, these happy subjects and servants of King Yah, soon have to come under the reign of King Beel?

The whole city began to rush toward the Palace. The Palace servants were at first afraid to go to the Throne Room. How could they tell King Yah? How would he take the news? Slowly, the servants began to realize that King Yah, who was in constant touch with the Prince through their mysterious communication, must surely know about his death.

Quietly, they made their way to the Throne Room. They must share this most awful time with him. They must see their King. As they approached the big room, they could hear voices. The King and Ambassador were talking. Now the King knew. The Ambassador had come. He had brought the news, that terrible news, about their lovely Prince.

The King's Surprise

The Throne Room was placed in the center of the Palace. Without permission from the Prince, none of the subjects were allowed into that room. The Palace servants, of course, were allowed into the room to serve the three rulers.

Once a year, one man who had been appointed by the King to gather all the offenders of the laws of the land would come into the Throne Room to present to the King the list of offenders and the crimes that had been committed. The King then provided a way that all the subjects could come back into his good graces.

The Ambassador was there in the Throne Room with the King. The King demanded justice. The Ambassador demanded mercy. Together, these rulers kept such harmony that the whole world knew of the peace and serenity in the Kingdom of Light.

The King's Surprise

The Prince, before his fateful trip, had been seated on the right hand of the King. The Ambassador was always standing, for he had to be ready at a moment's notice to go on a needed errand of mercy. There had once been a throne for him, too. But since he never seemed to sit in it but was constantly seeing to the needs of almost everyone, he had asked that it be removed. "I do not become weary when I am busy," the Ambassador had said with his big smile. Silently, often unnoticed, he went about his job of seeing that mercy was given to everyone in the Kingdom.

And so, enclosed with heavy curtains the three rulers had performed the duties of State in the great Throne Room. Outside the Throne Room was a hall with one small door. The hall encircled the Throne Room, the door led into another large room. In this room the City Fathers met. Meetings were held here. Here the King, Prince and Ambassador talked and mingled more freely with the people. Less serious matters of State were handled in the room. It was called the Inner Room.

There was also a very, very large outer room. This surrounded the other two rooms. There were gardens in this room and many couches and chairs. Here everyone was welcome to come. It seemed the Prince had spent most of his time in this outer room. It had become known as the Room of the Subjects, for it always had someone there who wanted to see the Prince.

The fearful, sad subjects had come into this outer room to mourn their Prince. The Palace servants had made their way from the outer room into the Inner Room. It was in the Inner Room that they had heard the King and Ambassador talking for they were in the Throne Room. Did the servants dare to go into the Throne Room? They wanted to be as close to their two remaining rulers as possible. They decided that they would stand in the hallway outside the Throne Room and outside the curtains. One by one the servants went through the doorway into the hall. One by one the servants would give a gasp in disbelief. Then he would step aside and fall to his knees.

The sight as they stepped through the door shocked each servant. The huge curtains that enclosed the Throne Room had been torn. They stood parted. There were the King and the Ambassador. But to the great surprise and shock of the servants seated on his throne at the right hand of his Father sat the Prince, as lovely and warm as ever!

A huge smile from the Prince greeted each servant who entered the door. The servants fell on their knees in worship and adoration to their beloved Prince.

How long this time of praise and worship lasted

no one seems to know. No one cared. The joy was unbelievable. The Prince was not dead! He was here! He had come home! Some of the servants cried. Some laughed. All were filled with an unspeakable joy. The Light was back! Their Light was here. The Prince had come home.

The Secret Plan

Their Prince had suffered untold agony at the hands of the peasants and King Beel. His wounds were still visible. There were large holes in each hand and each foot. Some sharp object had been nailed into his hands and feet. Then there was a large gaping wound in his side. Even though the servants knew the wounds were only a few hours old, they had completely healed. From the looks of the wounds and the size, all of the servants knew Prince Christos could not have lived through the agony that wicked King Beel had inflicted upon him. Yet there he was, alive and well and beautiful. Yes, beautiful, somehow more beautiful than anyone could remember him being.

The King stood. "My dear, faithful servants. How joyful we are to have our dear Prince back home with us. As all of you know, King Beel for many years has plotted the death of my son. When the Prince took his trip across the River of Death, King Beel thought that now at last he would be successful in killing my son. He felt, of course, with the Prince's death the Ambassador and I, too, would soon die of a broken heart because of our love for my son. What he did not know was that his ultimate victory would be, in fact, complete defeat for him and his Dark Kingdom.

"And so he plotted to kill my son. Today he completed his most wicked plan. You heard on the street the outcome of his plot. But my son is not dead. Why, no, for you see him here as radiant and fit as ever. Even his scars from the last few hours he has spent are like medals of victory.

"Now you may be asking, 'Why did our ruling Prince have to go through such pain and suffering?' The answer is quite simple. For as long as I can remember, I have desired many sons. I had often considered adoption. It would have been quite simple but for the law which stated, 'The punishment for rebellion against our glorious King is death.' Remembering this law has always brought a deep sadness to me. For I knew better than anyone that since the rebellion of King Beel each one of my subjects has been at one time or another rebellious. Even my most loyal subjects have confessed acts of rebellion. Yes, many were sorry and asked forgiveness. But with this law there was no forgiveness, only death. One by one my subjects fell into the trap of King Beel. Why, Adam Bloodman, my trusted gardener, was the first of my subjects to cross the River of Death. Soon all hope was gone. All my subjects had fallen prey to King Beel.

"Long before Adam had left, my son, the Ambassador and I had realized the law provided one way out for all my subjects. For the law states that if one man of the line and lineage of the King who had never committed one act of rebellion could be found and if he would voluntarily die for the people, justice would be served. If he would die, rebellion could be forgiven. In short, he would die for the rebellion of all.

"The Prince was very aware of this part of the law. When the rebellion of King Beel first began, my Son presented himself as the one to die for all the people.

"When Adam Bloodman crossed the River of Death, we held a secret meeting. There we decided to allow King Beel to carry out his most awful plans. Justice would be served. King Beel's victory we knew would mean his utter defeat. For everyone knows darkness can never conquer light.

"My son, the light of the world, has always been victor over darkness. Can darkness put out light? Never! Light dispels darkness. My dear servants, the defeat of King Beel and his kingdom is complete. We shall allow them to function for just a little while longer. During this time, the Ambassador will go into the dark kingdom in order to find anyone who would like to become my adopted son. Now, all men, women and children can come back into the Kingdom of Light, and, even more, a way for their adoption has been provided. At last I can have my greatest desire, many sons.

"Prince Christos' responsibility will be the training of the adopted children. He will teach them all the laws and the ways of the court.

"What a wonderful day this is! What a grand day for the Kingdom of Light. My son, Prince Christos, has provided victory for all men, yes, and so much more. He has provided for the adoption of anyone who desires to become my son. 'Whosoever will may come.' " (King Yah here was quoting from the Great Book of State.)

The servants burst into a shout of praise. "Praise to King Yah! Praise to King Yah! Praise to his son!"

Unbroken praise continued for many hours. Wise King Yah once again had been right. The Palace servants who were not a part of the adoption would never fully understand their three rulers' love for foolish, lowly peasants. But this was what King Yah wanted and they knew in the end his plans were always good, and so they rejoiced. They rejoiced because King Yah would at last have his sons. But mostly they rejoiced to have their ruling, wonderful Prince home again.

PART II

VICTOR MANN

Charis

The Prince was required to make one more short trip over to the Kingdom of Darkness. The poor peasants and the subjects of the Kingdom of Light were to be told about the Prince's great victory. As always the Prince's humility prevented him from coming with great pomp into the dark kingdom. Therefore, he went to a few dear and select friends. Their surprise was even greater than that of the Palace servants; but their praise and worship of Prince Christos were much the same.

Then Prince Christos was home to stay. He brought all of his followers with him from the Kingdom of Darkness into Light. The Ambassador was so eager to begin his part of the plan that he went into the Kingdom of Darkness within a few days. Soon many, many men, women and children began to cross the River of Death. They all came to accept the offer of adoption King Yah offered. The Kingdom of Light was again a happy, bustling and busy place. Years slipped by quickly. The Ambassador kept busy finding new sons for the King, the Prince with the training program for them, and King Yah with the general matters of State.

The Ambassador had been trying for some time to persuade one poor peasant to come with him across the River of Death into the Kingdom of Light. His name was Victor Mann.

Victor Mann is a good example of how a son was adopted and taught by Prince Christos.

Victor's story really begins when a young girl of fifteen or sixteen crossed the River of Death and came into the Kingdom of Light. Her name was Charis. For as long as Charis could remember she had been contracted by her parents to marry Victor. This arrangement was most agreeable to both Charis and Victor. As small children, they were constant playmates. As they had grown older, Charis came to deeply love the strong, handsome young man to whom she was engaged. Victor, in turn, came to adore Charis. She was small and very beautiful.

One day Charis happened upon an old man. He told fascinating stories about a Kingdom which lay across the River of Death. Charis had often heard stories about that awful place. But the stories the Ambassador told were completely different, they made everything there seem bright and good and clean. All of this was very different from the life she had always known. Though Charis' family was very wealthy compared with most of the peasants there in the dark kingdom, her life seemed to have no purpose. Oh, she was well aware of King Beel's promise to make all the peasants kings with kingdoms and power but she had always laughed at that idea.

"These poor peasants cannot manage their own lives. How will they ever be able to manage a kingdom? Why, they will have to become different people in order to accomplish all they have in mind." Charis had many times thought this to herself. She had never spoken it out, for in the Kingdom of Darkness any talk about change or "becoming a new person" was considered high treason.

Charis began to seek out the old man. She came to know him as the Ambassador. She became convinced that life in the Kingdom of Light was much more the way life should be. She talked to Victor about the Kingdom of Light only once. She had casually mentioned the fact that she was beginning to believe that maybe the Kingdom of Light was not the sinister place she had always heard that it was. "Maybe," she mused, "it would do us all some good to have our deeds exposed to some light."

Victor had exploded. He did not need any light.

He was doing all right. He knew what that wretched King Yah was up to. He wanted to change people. He wanted to make them different. He wanted to make them good.

"Bah," Victor had exclaimed sticking out his tongue. "I could not stand to be around someone

who was so good all the time. Oh, no! I have no desire to come to any light. I will stay right here in darkness if you don't mind. And you are very silly to be even talking about such things."

Charis had said no more to Victor. She continued to meet with the Ambassador. Though she did not know them personally, she was beginning to love King Yah and the Prince. She became sorry for her rebellion against them. She soon began to want to cross the River of Death. The only thing which held her back was her love for Victor. She did not want to leave him. Yet, she came to love King Yah more than Victor and so, one day, she left him. Charis crossed the River of Death and came into the Kingdom of Light.

So now they lived in two different worlds. How this saddened Charis! After coming to the Kingdom of Light her love for Victor had grown to large proportions. (Love grows exceptionally well in the Kingdom of Light. In fact, it is the Kingdom's chief product and export.) Daily Charis would come to the Palace. She would come at dawn. She would sit in the outer room, waiting to see the Prince. The Prince and Charis would talk about Victor and how much she wanted him to accept the King's offer of adoption and to cross over into the Kingdom of Light.

Together they would go into the Throne Room. Charis would plead with King Yah to do something soon, for she felt that she could not bear this separation another day.

This close association with the Prince and King Yah began to make changes in Charis. Soon she was beginning to understand things about the Kingdom of Light few people seemed to understand. More than once she would be invited into high level meetings to listen to plans of great importance simply because she was there in the Throne Room. To someone who did not understand the workings of the State, it would have seemed Charis was becoming a very great nuisance. She was always there in the Throne Room. If she were not in the Throne Room talking to the King and Prince, she was somewhere in a corner of the room studying the Great Book of State which contained the laws and inner workings of the government.

To the rulers she was a delight to have around. Indeed she was more than welcome. The more she came, the better they seemed to like it.

Actually, what had been openly announced but not really understood by many subjects of the Kingdom of Light had been understood by Charis. You could come into the Throne Room to see the King at anytime. You could stay as long as you liked. The only requirement was that you had to be brought in by Prince Christos.

One day, Charis came at her usual time at dawn to the Palace. Prince Christos was there waiting for her. "Come," he said. "My Father is waiting for you."

They went into the Throne Room. Each time Charis was taken into this great, beautiful room she was filled with a sense of awe and wonder. How could she who was once a lowly peasant now be welcomed by King Yah as a daughter? It was sometimes hard for her to imagine herself as a child of a King, an equal heir with Prince Christos. Coming into the Throne Room only increased the wonder of it all. As she entered the Throne Room on that special morning, new praise welled up in her. She knelt and praised the King for a long time.

Quietly, the King began to speak, "My dear, we have become so close. What will happen when Victor comes over into my Kingdom? You come to see me daily now but will you come when Victor becomes my son? What will happen when you have been given your heart's desire? Will you forget about me then?"

Charis thought for only a moment. Then she began to weep. "Oh, it is true! It is true! When I first began to come to the Palace I was so selfish. I wanted Victor here. I thought only of my love for him. I was so selfish. Now, though, I have come to love you so much that I no longer come just to plead for Victor. I come to be with you, Father. Oh, I know now that Victor will soon be crossing the river into the Kingdom of Light and that brings me joy. But I have come to love our times together. I do not ever want these times to stop."

King Yah smiled. "I knew this would be your answer. The Ambassador went into the Kingdom of

Darkness this very hour to get Victor. This time he will come with the Ambassador. Go, prepare yourself for Prince Mann. Then when you are ready, go to the river. You will meet Prince Mann there. Today he will enter the Kingdom of Light."

Victor

To describe the conditions of Victor Mann's life in the Kingdom of Darkness would serve no purpose. Briefly, he had come from one of the wealthier families. But they had had their possessions taken from them by King Beel when Victor was about ten years old. They remained subjects in the Kingdom of Darkness, and clung to King Beel's lie that one day they would become kings, too.

Even though Victor's family had no money, they had continued to hold their position in society. Victor's father worked for the government with Charis' father. This gave them some prestige and authority even if they were poor peasants. Life in the Kingdom of Darkness was a daily struggle just to stay alive. It made little difference if you were rich or poor.

Victor had gone to work at the age of sixteen in

a small fish shop near the river. The shop was owned by a Mr. Snort. Mr. Snort was a mean old man who seemed to dislike everyone. Victor hated working for him but had no choice for he had no training to do anything else.

The worst part about his job was that the shop was located near the spot where the Ambassador led the people across the River of Death into the Kingdom of Light. That meant he had almost daily contact with the Ambassador. He did not always speak to the Ambassador but their eyes always met. There was something so piercing about the Ambassador's eyes. They made Victor want to cry and laugh at the same time. Victor avoided the Ambassador as much as possible. Victor had watched Charis as she had crossed the river with the Ambassador. This had been a turning point in his young life.

"Good riddance," Victor had said aloud. "I was not too sure that I wanted to marry anyone, much less that ugly, freckle-faced girl." But he knew down in his heart that Charis was a very attractive young girl. She was not ugly, and the few freckles she had across her nose only added to her charm and beauty. He also knew he wanted to marry Charis more than ever. But how could he? She had gone to live another life. She was in another country. So the pattern for his life for the next few years was set. Al-

though he claimed loudly and with great vigor that he had never liked Charis anyway, in his heart he secretly began to look for a way to join her once again, even if he had to cross the river to get her and bring her back. At last he realized his search was in vain. He would never cross the River of Death. Why, everyone who went through that river had lost some part of themselves down there, and they came out completely different people. Victor knew this for a fact. King Beel himself had once come to Victor and told him so.

Victor had no desire to be different. He liked himself the way he was. He was doing all right for himself. He did not need King Yah, Prince Christos or even Charis.

Victor began to run with some rather wild lads shortly after he realized he could not marry Charis. All of these boys had one aim in life, to get the other fellow before he could get you. Each lad carried a knife. A knife was a great luxury for a young boy in this country of poor peasants. The streets of the Kingdom of Darkness had always been dangerous. The groups of young lads like Victor's gang made things worse. The situation had gotten so bad in recent years that King Beel had put a strict curfew on the streets and had stationed street guards to keep down the thieving and mischief.

Actually, Victor had no stomach for bullying

old men or hurting old women and small children. (This was the favorite sport of the street gangs.) He also never got involved in the street fights or the stealing. Because he was smarter than the other boys, he could always manage to save face with big talk. He never took part in the fights but lagged behind to egg the other boys on.

It bothered him that he had probably talked some of the boys into doing some things they may not have done before, but he could always convince himself that he was not to blame. That is, until those quiet days the Ambassador would come into the shop. He disliked the Ambassador, as everyone in the Kingdom of Darkness did, but the Ambassador insisted on coming in to see Victor.

This morning was bright and clear. Victor could plainly see the river as he cleaned the fish there in Mr. Snort's fish shop. Victor tried not to look at the river. That always made him think of Charis. No! This morning of all mornings he did not want to think about Charis.

The night before had been fun and wild. Now morning had come, and Victor was sick about the things which had happened. A boy, younger and smaller than himself, had been hurt badly in a fight. The other boys had run off leaving him there bleeding and perhaps dying. Victor and the others

The author I couldn't remember at your B'party was:
James   Patterson

NY Times Bestseller multiple times —

Give him a look on line

EASTER STOR[Y]
(To be made the even[ing...])

You need:

1c. whole pecans					zipper ba[ggie]
1 tsp. vinegar					wooden s[poon]
3 egg whites					tape
a pinch of salt					Bible
1c. sugar					wax pape[r]

Preheat oven to 300 (this is important-[...])

Place pecans in zipper baggie and let children [crush them] into small pieces. Explain that after Jesus was [beaten by] soldiers. Read John 19:1-3.

Let each child smell the vinegar. Put [...] that when Jesus was thirsty on the cross, he wa[s given vinegar.] 19:28-30.

Sprinkle a little salt into each child's h[and and then] into the bowl. Explain that this represents the [tears and] bitterness of our own sin. Read Luke 23:27.

knew that the street guards would show no mercy for this boy if he were found after curfew. He would be thrown into the dungeon or even killed if he were found. But the boys had not cared. They had gone off merrily to find better things to do.

Victor had come back later that night to check on the bleeding boy and to help him to get home. His stomach knotted as he remembered the blood and the guards. They had passed so close by them that if the Ambassador had not shown up from out of nowhere to show them a hiding place just in the nick of time, they would have been caught. After the guards had passed, the Ambassador had helped Victor take the boy home. Then the Ambassador was gone almost as if he had disappeared.

Victor sat on his stool. He put down the fish and began to look at the River. He was so empty inside . . . so lost.

The door opened and someone came into the shop.

The Mysterious Hill

Victor looked around. It was the Ambassador. Victor started out the back door. He recognized the Ambassador and did not wish to be placed in any uncomfortable positions today. He felt the Ambassador could see his thoughts and knew all about his wicked life.

Evidently the Ambassador saw Victor head for the back door. With lightning speed, he, too, went to the back of the shop. As Victor stepped out of the back door, the Ambassador was waiting. He caught hold of Victor's arm in a friendly fashion and cheerfully said, "My dear boy, I am so glad you left that dirty, smelly shop. We must talk, and I really cannot bear that smell."

"Why do I hate this loving, gentle creature?" Victor asked himself for the hundredth time.

Victor put on a contemptuous smile and said,

The Mysterious Hill

"Get away from me, you! I will not hear anything about your glorious King or wonderful Prince today. I have better things to do with my time."

"No," the Ambassador said. "Today you will listen and today you will see."

Victor stood perfectly still. Yes, he would listen. This voice had very gently given Victor a command, and Victor knew for the first time that he was dealing with a force, a power, a being far greater than he had ever imagined. He had often suspected this was not an ordinary old man. Now he knew it. He also knew today, this very hour, he would become different.

They walked in silence. The Ambassador was leading the way. They came to the only place in the Kingdom of Darkness where you could see the Kingdom of Light. It was a small hill. The Ambassador started up the hill. Victor immediately stopped. He knew this hill. He knew this spot. He would not go up there. He had heard stories about people who had. All the people who came to this hill came away changed. He thought about the people who had gone up and then had gone immediately across the River of Death. Charis had come here. She had seemed no more than curious about the Kingdom of Light, but after coming here only one time, she had crossed the river into the Kingdom of Light.

Victor then remembered the people who had

come but had decided to stay in Darkness. He thought about Mr. Snort, his boss. He had come only one year before. He came back home, but he was never quite the same. Could it have been his trip to this hill? Oh, he had always been mean and surly, but after coming to this hill he had become so much meaner. He never smiled any more, not really, that is. He had sort of a contemptuous snarl he gave to his customers, but not a real smile.

No. Victor would not walk those few steps up that hateful hill. He was not going into the Kingdom of Light. He was already sick about his wicked deeds. He did not want to become any worse. He would stay the way he was. He would not go up that hill.

The Ambassador had reached the top of the hill now. He stopped and turned. He did not seem at all surprised that Victor had stopped at the foot of the hill.

He called to Victor, "Victor, my boy, come up. You must see the view from here." The Ambassador's voice was most pleasant, but he had given another command.

Victor stared at the top of the hill. His feet began to move. He started to walk up that hill. He must go to the top of the hill. That was the place he would make his decision.

What Victor Saw on the Hill

Thoughts raced through Victor's mind as he slowly took those first few steps up the hill. For many years this hill had been regarded with superstitious fear. It had always been the place for executions. As long as anyone could remember, all criminals had been taken there to die.

"It seems strange," thought Victor, "no one ever noticed the perfect view offered from the hill into the Kingdom of Light." That is, no one had noticed before Prince Christos was carried up the hill and left there to die.

Victor did not know exactly why the hill was no longer used for executions by King Beel. "Could it be the fact that the Kingdom of Light can be seen from the hill?" Victor thought. He was not sure. In fact, Victor was not sure about anything right at that moment. Though he had not reached the top of the hill, he was beginning to see a blinding, piercing light coming over its crest. That light was hurting his eyes and fogging his brain. He could not seem to think clearly. Victor tried to put his arm over his eyes but this helped very little. Suddenly he was taken by a determination to go to the top of the hill. He must see where he was going. He could not shield his eyes any longer. He must see everything. His pace began to quicken. The light, though blinding and frightening, was pulling at him.

His mind began to race. "I must stop. I must think this thing through," he thought. "I must remember what King Beel has told us about the Prince's death."

Victor stopped short as he thought back. King Beel had said that the Prince had come to destroy life. A Still Small Voice spoke in Victor's heart, "I am come that you might have life. I am Life. I am the Way. I am the Truth."

"He came to bring wars and end peace," King Beel had said.

"Peace I give to you," the Voice spoke again, "not as the world giveth peace. My peace I give to you."

Victor looked into the light. It was all so clear, so simple. How could Victor have missed the simple truth? All these miserable years of believing lies.

"What a fool I have been," Victor began to laugh. He started running uphill.

At the top of the hill, Victor stopped. The light was no longer blinding him. The light was simply helping him to see the truth. Victor stopped laughing. His laughter turned to tears.

For there at the top of the hill, Victor saw for the first time what Prince Christos had done for him. The Prince had died for Victor Mann, a poor, miserable, ungrateful peasant. He had died to make Victor worthy of becoming a child of a King.

The Ambassador came close to Victor. As he did he began mysteriously to change. He seemed much younger now though as gentle and merciful as ever. Then Victor was taken aback by his hands.

There in his hands were nail scars. His feet, too, were scarred. Victor knelt at those feet weeping.

"How could a Prince, a King, love me? How could a King want me?" Victor spoke through broken sobs. Even as he asked the question, he knew that the answer could never be given. It really did not matter how or why the King, Prince and Ambassador loved him. All that mattered was that they did.

Victor looked up again. Now Victor knew for sure that this young, strong Being was the Prince. Victor spoke to him. "I have been most rebellious, Prince. Somehow I must make things right. Help me. I must speak to your Father. He must forgive me. I want him to forgive me."

Prince Christos reached down to take Victor's arm. That gesture was so familiar, so like the Ambassador, Victor was sure for a moment the Ambassador had returned. He was struck by the resemblance between the Ambassador and the Prince. It was almost as though the two personalities had become fused together by some miracle. Victor had only a moment to ponder that, for the Prince began to speak to him, "I have taken your request to my Father. You have been given a full pardon. The Palace servants and Kingdom subjects have already begun their rejoicing."

The fact that the Prince had never left his side occurred only faintly to Victor. Everything that was happening was too wonderful to take apart and examine. Victor Mann had entered a new life. He was a different person. The very thing he had feared the most had happened. Instead of being an awful, binding thing, it had set Victor free. He knew that he would never again have to be afraid. For now he was a child of the King.

Final Instructions

Prince Christos and Prince Victor headed down the hill toward the River of Death. They were joined by the Ambassador about halfway down the hill. The Ambassador said not one word but walked silently beside Victor. As the three walked, the Prince began giving instructions to Victor. "Now, Victor, you will find one thing my Father insists upon is truth. This really is not as hard as it may seem. Being in the Kingdom of Light helps everyone see the truth and know it.

"One thing I must tell you in all fairness and truth. Crossing the River of Death may not be easy. There is a set path. I will be on that path all the time. Whether your crossing and, indeed, the rest of your life will be easy or hard will depend on one thing—whether you stay on the path close to me. The closer you stay, the easier it will be. The more you stray from the path and me, the harder it will be."

Victor was struck by the Prince's honesty. He was sure he would have no trouble staying close by the Prince. Anybody could follow a small path and right now all Victor wanted was to be near the Prince.

Victor could not help but think about the difference the past few moments had made. He had always been plagued by a deep fear of not being understood. All that was gone. He knew the Prince and Ambassador understood him. After all, the Prince had anticipated his fear of the river and had explained how to cross the River of Death.

Victor Mann was truly a new man. A new heart beat in his chest. He felt like a little babe, all clean and pure and new.

He looked over to the Prince. "Can this really last?" he thought. "Am I actually to become a son of the King?"

Prince Christos turned to Victor. "We will soon be down the hill. I must caution you against something. In the Kingdom of Light, if you rely too much on your own understanding, you will become confused. There is a key to your new life. It is faith. In my Father's Kingdom it comes alive. It is a way of life. You will come to live by faith. You will come to have complete trust and reliance in and on my

Father. I have promised you that you are an adopted son of King Yah. You must only believe this. Then as you accept and believe by faith, you will find all your questions will be answered."

Victor smiled. "I am going to have to get used to having someone who knows my thoughts," he murmured under his breath. He did not want the Prince or Ambassador to hear him. Then Victor's eyes met the Prince's. They both began to laugh. Together they started to run down the hill to the river.

The River of Death

"The River of Death has always been a fearful place for me. Even as a child, I did not want to get too close. I was afraid that I might fall in. On top of the hill, it seemed that crossing the river would be easy. Now I am again afraid."

The Prince sat down on a rock beside the river. "Do you know why you have always been afraid of the river?"

"No," said Victor.

"Well, I do. Look across the river. Look as far as you can. Can you see the other side? Can you see the Kingdom of Light?"

"No," answered Victor, "all I can see is that heavy fog that always hangs there in the middle of the river."

"Victor, the River of Death is just that. All who cross the river will die. What is death? It is to give up your life or to lose your life. You must give up one life and cross into another. Now, Victor, you did that back on the hill. You gave up your old life and came into the Kingdom of Light. You will cross the River of Death but you will not die. You are already dead. How can a dead man die?"

The Prince smiled that wonderful smile as he got up. He reached for Victor's hand. "Remember, stay close by me. I will be walking on the path. I know the way. Because I know the way, I am the only way you can cross the river.

Together Victor and the Prince stepped into the river. Victor held tight to the Prince's hand. A sudden fear gripped Victor's heart. He quickly looked to the Prince. Prince Christos smiled and said, "My grace is sufficient for you." Victor knew he could depend on the Prince and so he moved even closer to him.

The dark, swirling waters had come up only to their knees. The Prince gripped Victor's hand tightly. Then he let go of it. He said, "Watch me." Just then the Prince stepped into a rather large drop-off. He was up to his chest in the water. Victor was still in the knee-deep water. He began inching his way to the drop-off. The water around the Prince swirled. It wet his hair and splashed into his eyes. "No, Victor, not that way. Take my hand. I will help you make that step down."

At this point, Victor made a big mistake. He began to doubt that the Prince knew how to cross the river. Though Victor had never crossed any river, he did not think that this would be the best way to get down. He began to feel for the bottom of the river instead of taking Prince Christos' hand.

"I will find the bottom and the edge of the drop-off. Then I will sit down on the edge and ease myself into the deep water," thought Victor.

Prince Christos stood silently. He still had his hand extended even though he knew that Victor was trying to find the bottom of the river on his own. He knew what was going to happen next for he stepped back one step as the current caught Victor. He went plunging headfirst into the water.

Even though the water came only to Victor's chest he had never been in a river. However, even if he had been an experienced swimmer, the turbulent waters of this river could have meant death.

As Victor lost his balance and went plunging into the black, swirling water a sinister voice from nowhere spoke. Victor recognized the voice of his former master, King Beel. "See, you fool! He got you into the river only to kill you."

Victor was, indeed, in a terrible situation. He was under the water now. He tried to fight his way to the surface. Where was the Prince? Had he gotten him into the river only to see him drown? No! Victor

could never believe that. Yet here he was on the bottom of the river and he was about to drown. "Oh, Prince Christos, help!" Victor thought. Then a strong hand grabbed his. Instantly, he was out of the deep water and back into the knee-deep water.

Again the Prince extended his hand to Victor. This time Victor grabbed his hand and was slowly eased into the deep water by the Prince.

"Lean on me, Victor," instructed the Prince.

Victor leaned on the Prince as they slowly inched their way across the river. Before he knew it, they were in the thick fog in the middle of the river.

Prince Christos spoke to Victor, "In a moment we will be on the other side of the fog. Lean on me, for we will be under the water for a few seconds. After a few more steps there will be another drop-off. I know where it is and I know how to get through this part of the river. I know how to get you through, too."

Victor did not want to fall into deep water again. He determined in his heart that no matter what took place, he would lean on the Prince. In fact, he grabbed the Prince's arm. The Prince laughed and stopped walking. "No. Do not grab my arm. I will hold you. You must only lean on me. Trust me. Lean on me."

Victor let go of Prince Christos' arm. He put his whole weight on the Prince's chest. He could not feel the Prince holding him. He did not feel anything. So he leaned harder on the Prince.

As he and the Prince went under the water, he sensed that a strange, wonderful thing was happening. Though he could not feel the Prince at all, he knew that the Prince was there. He knew that the Prince was guiding him safely to the other side.

"This is faith," the Still Small Voice spoke from within Victor.

Victor still does not know how long they were under the water. It must have been only a few seconds though it seemed longer. Victor was being changed. He became aware his old life was dead. He was entering a new and wonderful life. He was going to a new place as a new man. The water seemed to show the death of his old life. "This will show King Beel that I am no longer part of his kingdom," thought Victor.

Then Victor felt his feet drag the ground.

A hand reached for his and he was standing in knee-deep water again. He stood there for a few minutes getting his balance. The river had completely changed. The pulling current was gone. They were on the other side of the fog now. Now the river was crystal clear and very warm.

"In the Kingdom of Light the river is the River of Life," Prince Christos said.

Victor looked up. The city that lay before him

gleamed and glistened. Never had Victor seen a more magnificent sight. It seemed the whole city glowed with a strange and supernatural light. "It is beautiful," Victor exclaimed. "Everything is beautiful."

Hand in hand the Prince and Victor walked to the shore of the river. Even as going under the water seemed to symbolize the death of Victor's old life, coming to the shore of the Kingdom of Light seemed to show that Victor was a new man.

Once he reached the shore he fell down completely exhausted by the water and his experience. He was laughing and weeping. In a few minutes, he went to sleep.

PART III

PREPARING FOR THE WEDDING

Arrival at Joy Street

Victor just sat. He tried to remember that a bridegroom was supposed to be dignified and nervous but a joy would well up in his heart that was impossible to control. His smile could only be described as a grin. At long last his beloved Charis was to become his wife.

He had begun his preparations for the wedding feast early in the day. Now, he found he had done everything he needed to do. He had checked and rechecked everything. There was no more he could do. He sat down to meditate on the wonderful future prepared for him. Though he was quite alone, he said aloud, "If the next years are anything like the months since my crossing the river, I will not be able to contain my joy." Then he grinned and said, "But I shall surely try."

Victor closed his eyes and began to reflect on

the past months. Time is almost forgotten in the Kingdom of Light. For, as you know, there is no night there. The months slipped backwards and Victor was once again lying on the river bank asleep.

As Victor awoke, there was a sweet perfume that filled his nostrils. "Can it be? I dare not open my eyes. Could Charis be here?" thought Victor.

From the first time Charis had met with and talked to the Ambassador she had had this sweet fragrance. Victor had come to detest this sweet, delicate odor. For each time she met with the Ambassador, Charis was being drawn further and further away from him and closer to the Kingdom of Light.

Now Victor had come to the Kingdom of Light. As he lay there in the soft grass smelling that most delicate fragrance he dared not open his eyes but drank in the delightful smell that filled him with a strange sense of peace and joy.

Slowly he became aware of a pressure on his arm. He opened his eyes. His eyes met those still brown eyes that he had always loved.

Charis was beside him. Her hand was on his arm. "She is far more beautiful than I dared to remember," he thought.

Charis jumped up. She began to laugh and clap and dance around him. She was like a princess as she danced. Charis reached down. She grabbed both of his hands. Together they danced in a childlike way

around and around laughing and then crying together.

They sat down exhausted. Breathlessly, Victor blurted out, "How did you know? Were you surprised to see me here?"

"Oh, no," Charis said, hardly able to talk from joy and dancing. "I have known for months now that you would be coming. I just did not know when. Then King Yah told me this morning that the Ambassador had gone to get you. Oh, Victor! You are going to be so very happy here. The King is most loving. Everything is more wonderful than anyone can imagine."

"I cannot imagine anything more wonderful than this very time," Victor said as he took Charis' hand.

For several hours, they stayed by the river laughing and talking. Though there is no night, a soft sleepy dusk falls on the Kingdom of Light each day. As dusk began to come, Charis took Victor's hand.

"Come. There is a home prepared for you. This life is so new and different. We have many things to learn."

Charis took Victor to a small cottage situated on Joy Street. "All new arrivals to the Kingdom live on Joy Street for a time," Charis explained. "You will be living with a young couple who have been in the

Kingdom for quite a few years. They will help you to adjust to your new life."

Victor knocked on the door and a handsome young man came to the door. Victor could tell from first glance that he would like this man. Charis introduced him as Mark Helper. Mark gave Victor a huge bear hug and ushered him into the small well-lit cottage.

Charis called to Victor just before the door was shut, "Have a blessed rest."

"Imp" Patient

All life in the Kingdom of Light revolves around King Yah. This is quite different from life in the Dark Kingdom, for in Darkness each person lives only for himself.

Victor was able to easily and quickly adjust to this new life style for several reasons. First, he really loved the three rulers. He made daily trips to the Palace. Each day began and ended with a long visit with the Prince. Many times during the day he would look up from his work bench and look at the Palace using that strange communication provided by the Ambassador. In this way he could stay in contact with the Prince all during the day.

Victor had begun working with Mark Helper. Mark was a cobbler by trade. He had a shop there in his small cottage. Victor was a willing worker and an able apprentice. Mark's business was to see that

"Imp" Patient

each foot in the Kingdom was shod with the preparation of the gospel of peace. Victor's new profession and close contact with Mark was the second thing that made his adjustment easy.

Victor's new work was not easy. He spent many hours in the shop. Mark believed each person in the Kingdom was very special. Thus each person must have a special pair of shoes. Victor loved this work and was beginning to take as much care in the fitting of the shoes as Mark did. This required knowing and loving each person who entered the shop.

Perhaps that is why Victor became easy prey for a young man named "Imp" Patient.

Victor's life had been moving smoothly and quite on schedule. Then the day came when he met "Imp" Patient. "Imp" was not his name, of course, only a nickname. Actually his name was Verry but that did not seem to fit his disposition. So someone gave him the nickname "Imp" and the name just stuck. In fact, he had been "Imp" for so long most of the subjects had forgotten his name was really Verry.

"Imp" came into the shop one day not looking for shoes but only wanting to pass the time away. Mark had learned several years ago not to entertain this lazy young man and had cautioned Victor to leave him alone. "Leave him to King Yah," Mark had said. "The King has wisely assigned him a job and he is supposed to be staying with a distant cousin of mine. He is an older man named Matthew Helper. Yet 'Imp' will not stay still long enough for Matthew to help him. Of late, 'Imp' has refused to work or to stay with my cousin. Take my advice and let him be. He has no interest in our shoes. He will soon leave the shop."

Just then "Imp" smiled at Victor and said, "You're new here, aren't you?"

"Yes," Victor smiled back. Victor could not understand Mark's attitude about this young man. Mark took extra time with everyone. Now this young man who needed help had come into the shop and Mark did not even want to talk to him. If he really was not doing what King Yah wanted him to do, then he needed someone to help him.

"I will only talk a few minutes. Perhaps I can assist him. I have been able to help others, Mark. You have said so yourself," Victor told Mark as he strolled to the front of the shop where "Imp" was standing.

"I wouldn't if I were you," Mark said. "But I guess you have to learn for yourself."

Mark left the shop to make some important calls and an immediate conversation and friendship was struck between Victor and "Imp."

Several days passed. Each day "Imp" came into the shop and the two young men would talk. Victor

"Imp" Patient

found that "Imp" had many, many plans. Some of them were quite good. Each day "Imp" would come into the shop with another elaborate plan of some sort. He seemed to know something about everything. He had a plan to rework the water system. He had worked some with street repair and he had some very good ideas about how that work should be done.

"Imp" seemed to be interested most of all in Victor's and Charis' wedding plans. Victor and Charis had agreed with King Yah that their wedding would take place about one year after Victor's arrival into the Kingdom of Light. This would give Victor time to adjust to his new life. The delay most importantly though would give Victor time to attend a seminar on marriage. Being a husband is an important position in the Kingdom of Light. It is not a position to be entered without training. "A husband must understand his place in the Kingdom," King Yah had advised him.

All this seemed reasonable and right. That is, until "Imp" became Victor's friend. His constant questions and probing kept Victor's mind in a whirl. To answer one question only meant he would come up with another one. Then "Imp" would laugh good-naturedly and say, "I wouldn't wait if I were you. There is no time like the present, I always say. Why, if a beautiful creature was going to be my wife, I would never wait."

Mark Helper never mentioned "Imp" to Victor again though in a short time they became constant companions. From the day "Imp" walked into the shop Victor became more and more like his new friend.

One day as he and Charis walked by the river bank, Victor blurted out, "I want to be married!

Now! We will have our wedding tomorrow! I have waited long enough. I will not wait another day!"

Charis had noticed the subtle change that had overtaken Victor. She did not like it and was most annoyed with Victor and his new-found friend. She was convinced "Imp" was responsible for Victor's recent attitude. Therefore, she flung her head around, put her hands on her hips and snapped, "We will not! I am not about to marry someone who does not even understand what marriage is all about!" With that she stormed away but not until she had added in her most curt voice, "Anyway, I may *never* marry someone who is so friendly with that 'Imp' Patient! So there!"

Victor was stunned and hurt. He yelled to her as she stormed away, "I will be friends with whomever I please!"

As dusk fell, Victor did not feel like resting or talking. "Imp" came by as usual. Victor was too upset even to be with him. "I am going to the Palace. I have not been there in days. Come and go with me. I must talk with King Yah."

"No, thanks," he said, "I plan to go later today but I cannot go now. I do not really have time to talk. I am in a hurry. I just thought you may have had something happen today. Heard any new word about your wedding plans? I tell you, I cannot wait. . . . "

Victor began to laugh, "You know, 'Imp,' you

can never wait and you are always in a hurry. Yet in the weeks I have known you I cannot remember your finishing one thing you started. You have a lot of big and important plans but you never finish anything. Now, I know even though you say you are in a rush, you will take up the rest of my day if I let you. Not today. If you want to come with me to the Palace, let's go. Otherwise, I am in a hurry."

Victor left "Imp." He was now more miserable than ever. But that Still Small Voice inside him kept saying, "Go to the Palace, quickly!"

Victor knew from the fragrance in the Palace that Charis was there too. He looked but he could not seem to find her. Then he remembered he had come to see the King. So he began to look for the Prince. Victor was in the outer court. He looked and looked. He could not find the Prince either. It seemed he had been away for weeks rather than a few days. A great loneliness swelled up in his breast. Victor fell to his knees. "Never again," Victor said, "shall I become so involved with anyone or anything that I forget to come to the Palace. Oh, Prince Christos, I am sorry. Do not hide yourself from me. I do need you."

"I am here, Victor," the Prince said. "Get up. We will go into my Father."

Outside the Throne Room was Charis. She saw Victor and the Prince coming. She ran to Victor.

"Oh, I am sorry, Victor. You see I am not ready to become your wife. I acted so rebellious. Please forgive me."

"Charis, there is nothing to forgive. It was I. I was the one to blame. Forgive me."

Together they walked into the Throne Room. There they knelt and talked to their Father. They had come from a place of separation. Now they found, just as they would again and again, there was unity, freedom and peace there before the Throne of their Father.

Victor Finds a Pet

One bright afternoon Victor had gone outside the shop for a walk in the fresh air. His walk had led him to the river bank. This was a favorite place for Victor. He sat down to look at the clear, blue, still waters. He had drawn his legs into his arms. His head was held high as he took in the beauty of that quiet time.

He was suddenly startled by something cold and wet on his hand. There sitting beside him was an adorable, little dog. Victor laughed at him for the dog wagged his tail and looked lovingly at Victor. "My, you are a tiny puppy," Victor said.

He was obviously hungry and wanted to be fed. Victor had taken some bread and figs with him on his walk. He drew a few scraps from his cloak. He gave them to the dog and took up a little time with him.

Victor Finds a Pet

The dog followed Victor home. Soon like all dogs which are fed and played with, he belonged to Victor.

Actually this beast was not really a dog at all. But it was as innocent as a pup to begin with, full of fun and pep. At this puppy stage it is really hard to tell they are not dogs. As they grow they become more and more vicious. They have long fang-like teeth as long and sharp as a tiger's and huge, sharp claws. Most of them are found in the Kingdom of Darkness. In Darkness some owners allow them to even run wild. Most of the owners tell themselves they keep these dogs under control very well. Though they have harmed others too, it is strange that it is their masters they normally attack. They have been known to break their chains or cages and actually devour their masters.

Victor had acquired this dog almost innocently. But when the Still Small Voice told Victor to leave the pup alone, he refused. How could something so tiny and cute be harmful?

At first Victor kept the pup a secret. He carried him in his cloak. He gave him bits of food here and there because these dogs are always hungry.

Then he could keep the pup a secret no longer. He put him in his room and lovingly brought scraps of food regularly to him. Oh, how Victor loved that puppy.

When Mark Helper told him he should get rid of it, he was very hurt. "How can anyone not like this cute little thing?" Victor asked.

"But it is not a dog. These are not allowed in the Kingdom of Light. It will only cause you grief and pain. Destroy it, Victor, before it becomes too big and tries to destroy you."

"You do not understand anything, Mark. I will keep him outside on a chain if you like. But I will not destroy him. He is too cute."

Victor took sticks and leaves to make a shelter for his dog. They played and romped. "I must give you a name," Victor said to his dog as he chained

him to a tree near the shelter he had built. "I know you are greedy so that will be your name. I will call you Greed."

Each day Victor took special joy in seeing how fast Greed was growing. His fangs had begun to grow now and his beautiful, golden coat had turned gray and became matted. He would growl and show his teeth at Victor when he came near him.

This dog was no longer a pet but Victor still loved him. He was even more determined to keep him. He spent an increasing amount of time with Greed. He could no longer romp and play with him. So he would only sit and watch him eat.

Greed had been satisfied with scraps when he was a puppy. Now he had grown into a big dog and he demanded the best of food. He would refuse to eat anything else.

Victor had to satisfy the hunger of this big, ugly beast. He made little money working for Mark. So he decided to get another job. This job was hard to find. He spent many days looking for work. In the meantime, Greed was getting bigger and so was his appetite.

Victor did not really want King Yah or the Prince to know about Greed. It did not occur to him that they knew about his innermost secrets. He would come to the Palace each morning but leave early in order to feed Greed. He had almost decided to go back to his old profession in a fish shop. He had gone so far as to send across the river for his old fishing net. The day the fishing net arrived he had gotten another job working in a vineyard owned by King Yah. The net had smelled so terrible that Victor had hung it outside near where Greed was chained. "I will keep this, just in case I need it some day," Victor had told himself.

Now Victor was working at night too. King Yah had needed a watchman for his vineyard. With his work at the cobbler's bench and the night watchman's job, he had no time for his visits to the Palace. Victor had explained to Prince Christos that he had a real desire to do more for King Yah. Therefore he had taken this job at the vineyard. The vineyard belonged to King Yah. Victor was sure that King Yah could not object to this new job because he was, after all, working for the King. "Because I must work, I will not come in the evening to the Palace," said Victor, "but you know where to find me should you need me."

Victor did not seem to realize he needed the King, Prince and Ambassador. They did not need him.

A Close Call

Though Victor went faithfully to the Palace each morning, he had not seen the Prince in days. He did not really want to see the Prince, that took too much time. One thing Victor did not have these days was time. He hurried home each day relieved he had not run into the Prince or King. Victor had forgotten a conversation he and the Prince had once had. The Prince had said, "If you seek me, you will find me. I will always be there. I will not impose myself on you though. You must seek me. Those who do not want to see me, will not."

Victor had been stunned. "How could anyone not want to be with you. Why I, myself, have learned so much from you. I shall always want to be near you."

This had completely slipped Victor's mind since Greed had come into his life. He had been so involved in satisfying his dog that many things he had learned had slipped his mind.

"Greed, you are eating me out of house and home!" Victor had told his dog one day. Victor had laughed but a gnawing in the bottom of his stomach told him it was true.

The Helpers had been more than patient and kind. They even seemed to understand Victor's attachment to his dog. They hated the dog but they loved Victor. Therefore, they put up with the ugly, dangerous beast.

"The dog must go," Mark had finally told Victor. "We love you and want you to stay but you must destroy that beast. He is dangerous."

"Very well. We will leave. Greed is not dangerous. I can easily control him."

Victor walked from the cottage. He did not know where he would go. He just knew that he must have Greed. He would not destroy him, not now.

Victor put some food near the end of the chain. Greed hungrily began to eat. Victor decided he would throw his old fishing net over Greed. Then he would unchain him and drag him out to the street. There Victor could decide what to do next.

While Greed was occupied with the food, Victor put the net over his back. Greed fell down immediately, rolled over on his back and began to whine and cry.

"Oh, there now, my good boy, do not cry. I will not hurt you. It will be all right." Lying there in the net Greed looked again like the innocent pup that had first begged for food.

Victor could not resist. He reached down and put his hand through the net to pet his good friend lying so helpless and pitiful.

He was going to reassure his pet again that everything would be all right when the beast lunged at him. His hair was standing on end, and his teeth and fangs were showing.

The only thing that saved Victor from Greed's vicious attack was his old fishing net. Victor was standing on the net, however, when Greed moved toward him. Victor's foot and hand became entangled in the net. "Oh, no," Victor screamed, "Mark! Help!" As Mark came toward Victor all he could see was the net, the dog and Victor hopelessly entangled. Greed's repeated attacks at Victor only tightened the net.

Victor was somewhat protected by the net but blood covered his face, arms and chest where Greed's fangs and claws had cut deep into his skin.

"Oh, help, Mark! Please help! He will kill me! Greed will kill me!"

Mark stood helpless. How could he help? It is well known these beasts can only be killed by their masters or Prince Christos. He ran into the

shop for a knife. He must try. He would try to kill the beast. He must save Victor.

Victor was being torn and cut. Greed's anger was heightened by the fact that he had been tied by the net. He seemed determined to destroy Victor.

Victor could not last much longer. He was bleeding badly. He called out, again, "Help, King Yah! Prince! Oh, please, please help!"

Instantly, the Prince was there. His appearance was fearful. He wore a shining white armor with a sword between his teeth. He glowed with a blinding light.

Victor fainted from fear and pain.

Mark had come back with the knife. At the sight of Prince Christos he fell to his knees to worship him. Mark had no fear for his friend now. Prince Christos had come. He could only worship and adore the Prince.

Wedding Bells

Though Victor did not see what happened next, he later had Mark tell him again and again.

As he sat waiting for the hour of his wedding, he thought again about the conquering Prince. Mark had told the story this way:

"When I rushed from the cottage, I thought you were dead. Blood was everywhere. Your foot and one arm looked as though they had been completely torn off. Then I saw the Prince. A more awesome and terrible sight I had never seen. He took the sword in his mouth. With lightning speed, he killed the beast. Then he took the sword and set about cutting the net. The net fell from your bloody body. He picked you up in his arms and turned to face me.

"The armor, sword and light melted away as in a dream. The Prince stood before me. 'I need water,' he said. 'I am going to the River. Come with me.' If I had not known that the Prince had you, I would have feared for your life. The Prince was not afraid, however, so I was not either.

"We walked to the River of Life. Prince Christos put your head on a rock and began to tenderly wash you clean. A wonderful thing happened as he washed the blood away. All the cut and torn flesh came together. At his touch, the cuts were made well. He washed you clean. Oh, Victor! How our wonderful Prince loves us!"

Mark and Victor would weep for joy as Mark retold the story.

Even now remembering the day brought tears of gratitude and joy to Victor. Victor sat prepared for his wedding. The year was up. King Yah was even now preparing for his wedding at the Palace. He would take Charis as his wife.

Victor had learned many things. He was still not sure of some things. However, one thing he did know. Prince Christos would always be there to meet his needs. Though Victor may not always be faithful, the Prince always would be.

Just then Mark came running into Victor's room. "The bells! Hear the bells. It is time. Arise. The King is prepared for your wedding. Your bride is waiting. Victor, you will have a magnificent life. You have a wonderful, wonderful Father. After all, you are a son of King Yah."